This book
belongs to:

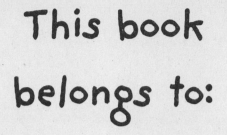

D0668865

•••••••••••••••••••••••••••••••••••••

•••••••••••••••••••••••••••••••••••••

The Batty Cat

and other stories

Written by
NICOLA BAXTER

Illustrated by
SASCHA LIPSCOMB

p

This is a Parragon Book
This edition published in 2002

Parragon
Queen Street House
4 Queen Street
Bath BA1 1HE, UK

Copyright © Parragon 2000

ISBN 0-75259-494-x

Produced for Parragon by
Nicola Baxter

Designed by Amanda Hawkes
Cover designed by Gemma Hornsby
Cover illustrated by Andrew Everitt- Stewart

Printed in Italy

Contents

The Batty Cat

People sometimes ask me why our cat is called Batty Cat. That just goes to show that they don't know our family very well and they don't know Batty Cat at all. You only have to spend ten minutes in the company of our cat to discover that he is well and truly batty. What other cat would try to catch the goldfish in the pond by swimming after them? What other cat would try to walk along the linen line? What other cat likes to eat old socks?

Batty Cat is a cat of mystery. No one knows where he came from. He simply turned up in our kitchen one day and never went away. Sometimes I wonder if somewhere there is a snorkelling, tight-rope-walking sock-eating pensioner just waiting for Batty Cat to come home, but the thought is too horrible. On the other hand, it's hard to imagine Batty Cat with a family any saner than ours.

But then, if I'm being truthful, our family isn't very sane. Mum painted the house purple last week. Dad has a massive collection of old phone books. Mags, my little sister, is totally bonkers—the way that only little sisters can be. Batty Cat, as you can see, fits right in.

When Batty Cat arrived, it was pretty obvious that he had already lived quite a life. His nose was scarred, he had a chunk missing from one ear, and there was a kink in his tail that suggested he had once caught it in a car door or something. We didn't think much about this until he lost his first life with us. You know how cats are supposed to have nine lives, losing one each time they have a narrow escape? Well, Batty had a narrow escape about half an hour after he arrived in our kitchen.

It was a Saturday morning. Mags was keen on acrobatics at the time and was hanging upside down from the kitchen door frame. Mum was having one of her enthusiasms for healthiness and was busy cooking something brown and solid on the stove. During these times, everything we ate was brown and solid. Mum had to tell us whether she was offering us beef

stew, chocolate cake or nut roast. It didn't make any difference. They all tasted like cardboard.

At the table, Dad was trying to build one of his matchstick models. That's his other hobby—phone books and matchstick models keep him occupied all the time that he's at home. He doesn't even watch telly, which is embarrassing when you're with friends and he asks, "What's a Klingon?"

I was cleaning my football boots. I sometimes think I'm the only normal person here. I play football. I watch football. I read football magazines and eat football-shaped cereal. And you needn't even think about offering me a drink if it's not in my red and white mug.

Anyway, I was cleaning my boots at the sink and quite a bit of mud was flying into Mum's cooking, but when something is brown and solid already, a bit of mud doesn't make a lot of difference.

As far as I remember (it all got a bit confused for a while), Mum bent down and took a large tin of something the colour of liver and the consistency of concrete out of the oven. She was carrying it across the kitchen, and I swear I was only practising a free kick with the shoe-cleaner can, when she suddenly crashed to

the floor. The tin of gunk flew up into the air, smashed the light bulb and hurtled down again. None of us noticed to start with that it landed with a sort of *thunk* instead of a crash on the tiled floor, as we were all looking at Mum.

Our mother isn't the most graceful woman in the world. She's constantly falling over something or off something or into something. So we didn't really think she had hurt herself, but it's only right to look up when your mother hits the deck. In fact, she was on her hands and knees, peering under the fridge and saying, "It must be three years since I cleaned under there, but I don't feel like doing it now."

We all went back to doing what we were doing, until Mags, coming down from a sort of somersault, suddenly cried out, "Oh, Mum, you've killed the cat!"

"We haven't got a cat," said Dad. But we had. Somewhere in the confusion, Batty had entered our lives and was now lying very still on the kitchen floor with a tin of something brown and solid on his head. He certainly didn't look lively.

Mags and Mum crouched over the body while Dad and I stood about feeling awkward. You can't just carry on when there's a dead cat in the middle of your kitchen, but on the other hand, we didn't see what we could do about it.  Dad shut the back door, perhaps thinking we could only deal with one dead cat at a time and it would be best to avoid any more of them turning up their toes in our old kitchen.

Very gently, Mum lifted the tin off the cat's head, and the cat gave a little groan and a sigh.

"It's alive!" cried Mum and Mags together, as if they were in a hospital drama on telly. The cat moaned and sighed again, and I don't know what it was, but maybe the thought of telly programmes put it into my head. I suddenly felt that the moan and the sigh were fake. That cat was acting! When he did the moan and sigh a third time, and put one paw over his forehead, I was certain. I went over and peered down at him. Slowly, he opened one yellow eye. I'm quite sure he winked.

Anyway, Mum and Mags spent the rest of the day running around after the cat, taking him to the vet, feeding him milk and sardines, and generally making a fuss of him.

"You can't practise football in the hall," they said, "you might hurt the cat."

"You can't watch the match," they said, "the cat needs peace and quiet."

"You can't have your supper yet," they said, "we're still looking after the poor little cat."

It's amazing that I didn't start hating that cat there and then, but even at the beginning I had a grudging admiration for him. I mean, he was milking it (if you'll excuse the term) for all he was worth. Mum and Mags decided to call him Patrick, because it happened to be Saint Patrick's Day. That was before we all knew quite how batty he was.

Later that evening, Pat the cat was well enough to wander around and get his bearings. At first Mum and Mags followed him everywhere, to make sure he was all right. After a while, since he was doing normal cat-like things, such as sitting on the beds and digging his claws into the sofas, they left him to it. Mum made supper at last and for once it wasn't brown and solid. As we were running so late, she opened some tins and we had something orange and squelchy instead. Then, after some prompting from me, she threw my football kit into the washing machine for the match the next day and rushed off to take Mags to her gymnastics class.

I don't know what made me go into the dark little passageway where the washing machine is kept. I think I was looking for an old pair of boots. As I passed, I happened to glance at the machine, which was just starting to fill and spin. A furry little face was pressed to the glass.

Well, I stopped the machine and opened the door as quickly as I could, flooding the passageway with water and ruining my old boots for ever. The cat came out in a rush with the water and half skidded under the boiler.

This time, I thought he was dead for sure. When I picked him up, he was limp and wet. He looked half his normal size with wet fur. I once saw a programme where a farmer tried to revive a newborn kitten by rubbing it in a rough towel, and that was all I could think to do. I picked up the cat and hurtled up the stairs with it and into the bathroom. Then I rubbed it as hard as I could and tried holding it upside down to get the water out. I've since been told I did all the wrong things, so please don't try it at home, but by sheer luck Pat the cat started moving. In a minute or two, he sat up in the towel and shook himself.

He looked absolutely fine. I carried him downstairs and laid him, still wrapped in the towel, on the sofa to recover. Then it was my turn to do the milk-and-sardines routine. Only…

While I was in the kitchen, Dad came into the living room and sat down to look at one of his telephone directories.

When I came back into the room, carrying Pat the cat's snack, there was no sign of him.

"Where's the cat?" I asked.

"He wasn't here when I came in," said Dad. I knew I had shut the door. A horrible suspicion began to grow in my mind as I looked at my father.

"Dad," I said, trying not to panic, "just get up for a moment, would you?"

Dad could see I was serious and heaved himself to his feet. There on the sofa was the towel. In the middle of the towel were two little ears. But the towel didn't move.

This time, I thought the cat must really be dead for sure. My dad's not a small man, and our sofa isn't particularly squashy. But a second later, the cat lifted its head and gave a little yowl.

Dad and I spent the rest of the evening taking the cat to the vet (again). The vet looked at us strangely, as if we were the kind of people who made a habit

of concussing, drowning and squashing cats, but in the end he said there was nothing really wrong and let us take him home. Pat the cat stretched out in the box we brought him in and settled down to sleep.

That evening, when Mum and Mags were back from gymnastics, we called a special family meeting to talk about what to do with the cat. Most of us had done him some damage at some time during the day, so we felt responsible for him. It was

decided that we would put up notices in
the local shop, and if no one claimed him,
we would keep him. It was sometime during
the meeting that Mags started to call him
Patty Cat, and the rest of us called out at
once, "No, let's call him Batty Cat!" The
name stuck.

It was also during that meeting that
Mags brought up the subject of a cat's nine
lives and how many Batty had left.

"He used up three this afternoon," she said. "That means he only has six left."

"From the looks of him, he's used up quite a few already," said Dad. "His scarred nose, his kinky tail and the chunk out of his ear must account for another three lives at least."

"The vet said he'd already had quite a few bumps and bashes," said Mum. "I doubt if he's got any lives left at all."

But Mags couldn't bear that. She claimed that he was a special cat, with not nine but nineteen lives, and she looked so eager that we agreed with her. By the end of his first day with us, we reckoned, Batty was on his tenth life and counting.

Over the next few weeks, Batty Cat seemed to have suicidal tendencies. He tried climbing the chimney from the inside just before Mum lit the fire. He tried sleeping in the oven just before Mum cooked the supper. He even tried sharpening his claws on one of Dad's matchstick models, which caused Dad to hurl a phone book at him from across the room. It wasn't a good plan. The book missed the cat and smashed the model, damaging the section on Architectural Ironmongery at the same time. Batty fled.

As the weeks passed, Batty's quota of lives was getting used up pretty quickly. When he got his head stuck in the milk jug and almost drowned, he reached number nineteen. We all felt a sense of dread. Next time might be *it* for Batty Cat.

By now, of course, we couldn't imagine life without that animal. He did the most extraordinary things—diving into a trifle when Aunt Muriel came to lunch, eating Mum's most solid and brown inventions with enthusiasm, lying on the bonnet of the car with all four feet in the air—but we all felt that he was a most extraordinary cat. And we wouldn't know what to do without him.

At last Mags said what we were all thinking.

"It's like having something really horrible hanging over you," she said. "It's as if we're just waiting for something awful to happen. Why don't we keep an eye on him instead? So that it can't."

After that, we tried hard to keep a round-the-clock watch on Batty Cat. It proved to be impossible. How do you follow a cat who is walking along telephone wires? Who can stay awake while he prowls around the neighbourhood visiting his lady friends, especially the little tabby cat next door? After a week, we gave up.

Then something really wonderful happened. Batty Cat got run over by a car. It may not sound wonderful to you, and of course it wasn't much fun for Batty Cat, who gained another kink in his tail and a very sore leg, but we were delighted. Batty had used up not nineteen but twenty lives, and he was still with us. We didn't have to worry after all. Some cats obviously have hundreds of lives, and Batty was one of them.

Batty is quite an old cat now, although he still does daft things. He tried hang-gliding from Mags' kite. He tried highboard-diving into the watering can. He stole some snacks from the Doberman down the street and ate them in full view. He still eats Mum's cooking, although brown and solid things have now become greenish-yellow squelchy things, as she's become obsessed by vegetables.

Still, we all know that Batty won't be with us for ever, and until this morning we dreaded the day.

This morning, however, Batty came into the kitchen with something dangling from his mouth.

"Ugh! It's a rat!" cried Mags.

"Is it dead?" asked Dad, thinking of little teeth gnawing his matchsticks.

But it wasn't a rat. It was a kitten, a little striped kitten who looked exactly like Batty Cat. And it immediately tried to climb up the table leg and fell into Batty's sardines.

There is no doubt about it. Batty the Second has come to stay, and we couldn't be happier.

The Real Dog

When Thomas first said he would like a dog, his father said, "No! There will be no discussion about it, Tom. You are not having a dog and that's final."

The next time Thomas mentioned how wonderful it would be to have a dog of his very own, his father said, "No! I don't want to talk about it any more. We'll think about it when you are older."

The third time that Thomas raised the subject of a dog in the house, his father said, "No! One day you will be able to have one, I expect. But at the moment I know who would end up cleaning up after it and feeding it." (He didn't mean himself. He meant Thomas's mother.)

When Thomas suggested for the fourth time that a dog would be a really wonderful addition to his life, his father said, "No! No, no, no, no, NO! Well, all right then."

But that didn't mean that Thomas's difficulties were over.

"It's very important what kind of dog you choose, Tom," said his father. "I know a thing or two about dogs, and I can tell you that what you need is a *proper* dog. Not one of those little ratty things with short legs. You want something like a labrador, or a dalmatian, or a setter."

Thomas's mother sighed.

"A labrador, or a dalmation, or a setter will need to run for miles and miles each day," she said. "You won't have time to do it and go to school, Tom. I know perfectly well who will end up roaming the countryside with your pet."

"You'd enjoy the exercise," said her husband. "I simply won't have a dog in the house that reminds me of a hairbrush, no matter how cute he is."

"But…" said Tom.

"But…" said Tom's mother.

"That's my final word," said Tom's father. "And I have nothing more to say on the subject."

As it turned out, Tom's father had quite a lot more nothing to say on the subject. On Monday, he said there was no way he would ever be seen with anything smaller than a sheepdog. On Tuesday, he said that his mind was made up that the legs of a spaniel were the shortest he would consider. On Wednesday, he spoke quite favourably about corgis, which he said were owned by some very important people, so the shortness of their legs didn't count. On Thursday, he warmed to the subject of terriers and remembered fondly a little white dog owned by his favourite uncle twenty years before.

On Friday, when Tom's father was explaining to anyone who would listen that some small dogs had a great deal of spirit, Tom's mother suggested that they all go down to the Rescue Centre to see what kind of dogs were available.

"Yes, then I ... I mean we ... I mean Tom ... will be able to make a sensible choice," said Tom's father.

It was exciting being at the Rescue Centre. Thomas couldn't wait to start looking at the dogs, but first a lady with a clipboard asked them to sit down while she took some details and found out if they could offer a dog the kind of home it needed. The first part, when she asked for names and addresses was fine. When she got to the bit about what kind of dog they were looking for, things became a good deal trickier. Naturally, it was Tom's father who caused the trouble.

"We are looking," he said firmly, "that is, Tom is looking for a dog with long legs … but not too long."

The lady's pen hovered over her clipboard.

"Which would mean…?" she asked, with a puzzled expression.

"Medium legs," said Tom's father.

"I was hoping," said the lady, with a noticeably colder tone, "that you would describe the *temperament* you would prefer in a dog."

"Lively," said Tom's father.

"Quiet," said Tom's mother.

"Friendly," said Tom.

"You have discussed this, have you, as a family?" asked the lady.

"Definitely," said Tom's father.

"Sort of," said Tom's mother.

"No one asked me," said Tom.

The lady put away her clipboard.

"I think you should all come back when you have sorted out what you really want," she said.

Tom was almost in tears. He could hear exciting sounds of barking behind the swing doors. It was horrible to be so near and yet so far from his dream. His mother, seeing his face, saved the day.

"I hope that's not necessary," she said. "What we need is a nice, friendly dog that my son could look after by himself—with our supervision, of course. A small dog would be best, but one with plenty of character. We will do everything we can to give him a happy life with us."

The lady softened.

"Perhaps you had better go and see the dogs we have at the moment," she said. "We can meet back here in fifteen minutes. I can then tell you more about any dog you are particularly interested in."

They saw lively dogs with tails that wagged non-stop.

They saw shy, retiring dogs that needed to be cuddled.

They saw tiny dogs.

They saw huge dogs.

And they saw Rags.

"There he is!" cried Tom, as if he had know Rags all his life. "It's him! Look!" Dad, *please* don't say anything to upset that lady!"

Thomas's father was about to protest, but Rags put his head on one side so comically that he had to laugh instead.

"He's a very fine dog," he said. "And I can see that he's exactly right for you, Tom. Even if his legs still have some growing to do."

Luckily, the lady agreed that Rags *was* exactly right for Tom. She arranged to come around to inspect Tom's house the next morning. Then, if everything was in order, Tom could take Rags home.

All the way home, Tom's mother and father talked about the tidying and sorting they would have to do to make sure the lady was happy the next day. But Tom just sat in the back of the car with a big smile on his face.

"I know it will be all right," he said. "Rags was waiting for me. I could see that straight away."

Thomas was right. The lady was happy to see that the family had a big garden with a tall fence. She was pleased that Tom's mother had thought about where the little dog would sleep and Tom's father had put anything that could be chewed high up out of reach. That very same afternoon, the family went to collect Rags and take him to his new home.

It was as if the little dog had always been there. Within a week, none of the family could remember what it had been like to come home and not see a cheeky little face peering through the window. They asked themselves how they had ever managed to enjoy country walks without a naughty little dog to dive into ditches and chase squirrels.

As for Tom, he and Rags were the closest of friends. Tom told Rags all his troubles and all his dreams. And Rags

would put his head on one side and seem
to understand everything.

"It's really sweet to see them,"
Tom's mother told his father, as they
watched their son playing with Rags in the
garden one day.

"I know," said her husband. "I'm
glad to feel that I made the right choice."

For a whole year, Rags was part of
the family. Then, one awful August day,
something dreadful happened. A huge
truck, rattling too fast around a corner
near Tom's home, lost control and

smashed through the fence into the back garden. There was terrible damage to the fence, the flowerbeds and the garage, but none of that mattered to the family. Rags had been sleeping under a bench. Now he would sleep for ever.

Without Rags, the house seemed cold and empty. Everyone had the feeling that they would walk into a room and see his cheerful little face once more. But they didn't. Rags had gone.

After a few months, Tom's mother and father talked about what they should do. Tom was very quiet and pale these days. They were worried about him.

"I think we should get another dog," said Tom's father. "It's like falling off a horse. You have to get straight back on again. And besides, looking after a new dog would take Tom's mind off it. He really hasn't accepted that Rags has gone."

For once, Tom's father was right. When the little boy's parents gently told him of their plan, he looked shocked.

"Oh no," he said, "I don't think that Rags would like that at all."

"What do you mean, darling?" asked Tom's mother.

"There's only room for one dog in this house," said Tom firmly, "and that's Rags. I don't need another dog while I've got him."

Tom's mother and father tried to explain that Rags was not coming back. But the more they tried, the more Tom insisted that they were wrong. He started taking Rags for walks again. At least, he took Rags' lead for walks. Each morning he put out fresh water and biscuits. Each evening, he said goodnight to Rags and patted an imaginary head before he went upstairs for his bath before bed.

"I don't know what to do," Tom's mother told her husband. "It's just so sad. Do you think we should take him to see someone? I can't bear to think of him having to pretend like this."

"Let's give it a few more weeks," replied Tom's father. "One day he'll just forget to pretend, and then Rags really will be gone."

But Tom wasn't really pretending. There was a Rags-shaped place in his heart

that simply had to be filled. Life without
Rags was impossible to imagine. Only he
did miss being able to cuddle the warm,
wriggly little dog. He missed the feel of
Rags' rough little tongue on his cheek. He
even missed being told off about dirty
pawmarks on the knees of his trousers.
But he wouldn't let himself miss Rags.
Rags hadn't really gone. He knew that.

"I think you were right after
all about getting another dog,"
said Tom's father to his
wife one evening.
"We can't go on
like this, and I
miss having a
dog around the
place. Tom will
get used to the
idea, although it may take some time for
him to become fond of another one."

But Tom's parents didn't have to go out and find another dog. Another dog found them.

One night shortly before Christmas, Tom was watching a TV programme when he suddenly looked up.

"I can hear something outside," he said. "I'm going to look."

"It's dark, Tom," protested his mother, walking behind him down the hall. "You can't go outside in this weather."

But Tom was already opening the front door. He peered out into the snow, but there was nothing to be seen.

"I thought I heard Rags," he said softly, hanging his head.

Tom's mother knew that the moment had come to talk about it all.

"I thought you felt Rags was still in here with us," she said gently, closing the door. "He can't be out there, too."

"It isn't the real Rags here with us," confessed Tom, starting to cry. "He's never quite here. And sometimes now, I can't see him at all. You know, the first time I ever saw him, it was like I'd been missing him for years already. It's like that again now. I keep waiting for him to turn up again."

Tom's mother gave him a big hug and let him cry.

"I think you have to let Rags go, sweetheart," she said. "He had a happy time with us, but that happy time is past. Don't you think it might be time to be happy with another dog? It wouldn't be Rags, of course, but I'm sure we would all grow to love it just as we did with that naughty little dog."

"I don't know," whispered Tom. "It would have to be Rags again, you see. I mean, it would have to be a little dog that I sort of knew before I ever saw him. And I don't think that could happen again. I've been hoping that Rags has been waiting somewhere, waiting to come back to us."

"Let's go back and sit down," said his mother. "I'll make you a drink."

But just then, there was a little scrabbling sound from outside. Tom's mother saw the hope flare up in her son's eyes, and her heart went out to the little boy as he ran to the door.

There on the doorstep sat a little dog. It wasn't Rags. It didn't look at all like Rags. But somehow... Tom frowned.

"I'm not imagining it," he said. "I'm not. I'm not."

Then, all of a sudden, the visitor put his head on one side in a way that was so, so familiar.

The little dog trotted in through the front door and wiped his feet carefully on the doormat. Thomas knew then that he *must* be imagining it. Dogs *never* wipe their feet. But the little dog walked straight into the living room and settled down in front of the television. He turned to look at Thomas, as if saying, "Come on, I'm waiting for you."

Thomas sat down beside the little dog. Very slowly he reached out his hand. Under his fingers he felt a warm, soft, living, breathing body.

"Welcome back, Rags," he said.

The
Particular
Parrot

My Aunt Margaret is one of those people who is always helping others. When her next-door neighbour has a cold, Aunt Margaret is there with bowls of soup and advice about woollen underwear. When the local primary school asks for knitted teddy bears to sell on behalf of orphans on the other side of the world, my Aunt Margaret knits furiously for weeks. You can't sit down in her living room without squashing half a dozen bears in various stages of completion.

In one way, it's very good that she throws herself whole-heartedly into whatever she is doing. In another way, it can be a bit scary. I mean, would you think it was possible that someone could knit six hundred teddy bears in a month? When does she find time to eat?

Helpful as she is to anyone who asks, Aunt Margaret saves most of her energy for the oldest of her neighbours. If you're ninety, beware! Aunt Margaret will bring you food, do your washing, take your letters to the post and tidy your room—whether you want her to or not! I once witnessed a pitiful tug-of-war as an old lady tried to hold on to her oldest and most comfortable slippers.

"They're past it," Aunt Margaret said firmly. "They're a health hazard. Look at these nice new slippers I've brought you."

The old lady kept a fierce grip on her slippers with her gnarled fingers.

"They're my favourite slippers and I want to keep them," she said.

Aunt Margaret tugged in her turn. "What for?" she asked. "You can't wear them with holes like this in the soles. You'll fall over."

"I just want to *look* at them," said the old lady. "That's not dangerous, surely?"

Of course, it was an unequal contest. Aunt Margaret gained possession of the slippers and would not let go.

"I'll make us a nice hot drink," she said. "It will be soothing."

When she had bustled into the kitchen, the old lady turned to me.

"I don't want you to think I'm losing my marbles," she sighed. "Of course I don't want those wretched old slippers. I was about to throw them out anyway. It's just the principle of the thing. Your aunt is a lovely woman, but she does like to have her own way. And so do I!"

I quite often went with my aunt to see the senior citizens. I liked them. They had lots of interesting things to talk about and they very often had tins of toffees hidden somewhere. Also, they liked to have their rooms really warm, and I live with my brothers and sisters in a huge, draughty old house. I liked their snug rooms. I even liked the way they usually had the telly on. It's amazing what you can learn on daytime television.

There's only one big problem about getting fond of really old people, and that is that sometimes they leave quite suddenly, before you've had a chance to say goodbye. I don't mean that they die, although that does happen, of course. I mean that they go to live with sons and daughters, or move into homes. That's what happened to Harry Baggle.

Harry Baggle was a jolly old man with a white beard around his chin and no hair at all on top of his head.

"It slipped," he said, the first time he caught me peering at his face. Somehow, he always made me wonder if he'd put his head on the right way up. Some elderly people like you to call them Mr. or Mrs. or

Miss. Some of them like you to use their
first names, which are usually something
odd like Gladys or Ethel or Gilbert.
Harry Baggle had other ideas.

"Call me Cap'n," he said, the first
time I met him. "I've been used to it all
my life and I'm not going to be plain Mister
now. You can't teach an old sea dog new
tricks, you know."

"Aye, aye, Cap'n," I said, which
made him laugh.

Unfortunately, it turned out that Cap'n Baggle wasn't a pirate. He used to be in charge of great big oil tankers and cargo ships, taking them all around the world. He had lots of books about huge ships, the bigger the better.

Cap'n Baggle didn't have a proper doorbell. Instead, there was a great big brass bell hanging up outside. You had to give it a big push to make it ring. But that wasn't the most exciting thing about the captain. That was Parrot Perkins.

"I named him after a First Mate of mine," said the captain. "He had the most annoying habit of repeating everything you said to him. Of course, we do that on board ship to make sure an order has been understood. But when I said, 'Pass the mustard, Perkins,' and he replied, 'Passing the mustard, Cap'n,' *every time*, it really got on my nerves. I'm afraid Parrot Perkins here has the same habit, don't you old boy?"

"You old boy," repeated Parrot Perkins, putting his head on one side. He was a big grey parrot and really handsome. He had his  own perch in one corner of the room, but most of all he liked to perch on the back of the captain's chair. His huge claws had made rather a mess of the upholstery, which made Aunt Margaret go *tut, tut, tut* every time she came.

Cap'n Baggle and Parrot Perkins were inseparable. When Cap'n Baggle went outdoors, which was less and less as time went on, Parrot Perkins rode on his shoulder. They always drew a crowd when they went into shops, although they were banned from the local supermarket because the parrot ate most of the green-grocery section before they got to the tills.

Unfortunately, it was probably the fact that Parrot Perkins was a big bird that caused the problem. He perched on my shoulder once, and I didn't really like it. Part of me was worried that his great claws would do to my shoulders what he had done to Cap'n Baggle's chair. The other part of me was just overwhelmed by the weight of him. Those parrots are heavier than they look.

Cap'n Baggle, with his tanned, happy face (and his tanned, shiny head) always looked the picture of health. But he was nearly ninety and not as steady on his feet as he used to be.

"You have to balance differently on land," he said to me once, when he almost stumbled in the kitchen. "It's hard to get the hang of when you've been at sea as long as I have."

Of course, Cap'n Baggle had been on shore for nearly thirty years. He should have got his land legs by now, but I didn't think of that at the time.

One fine day, Cap'n Baggle and Parrot Perkins went shopping. The captain bought lots of fruit for his best friend. Maybe it was the weight of his shopping bag, or maybe it was the weight of Parrot Perkins, but when the pair reached the steps by the bus station, they both took a tumble.

Parrot Perkins flapped away with lots of squawks but no scratches. Cap'n Baggle wasn't so lucky. He had broken his leg and broken it badly.

"For a man of his age, that means hospital for several weeks at least," said Aunt Margaret. "We must go to see him and do what we can to help."

I'm quite sure she didn't have in mind the help that Cap'n Baggle asked for.

"You see," he said, sitting up in his hospital bed in red pyjamas and looking remarkably well, "the Animal Rescue place is looking after Parrot Perkins at the moment, and I know he'll hate it. For one thing, that place is full of cats, and if there's one thing Parrot Perkins can't stand, it's cats. He'll be driving them all mad in there. Could you take him home with you, Margaret, just until I'm well enough to come home?"

Aunt Margaret went pale. I knew for sure that she was thinking of her chair-backs and Parrot Perkins' big claws.

"I'm sorry, Harry," she said. (She never would call him Cap'n.) "I really don't think I have the time or the skill to look after a parrot. I wouldn't know where to start. You'll have to ask someone else, I'm afraid."

Cap'n Baggle sighed dramatically.

"They all have cats," he said. Then he put on a truly pitiful expression and sighed again. "I don't know how I can ever get well with Parrot Perkins always on my mind," he said. "I can't sleep. I can't eat. I can't do anything when I'm so worried about my old Perkins."

I thought for a moment that he was going to cry, for he buried his face in the bedclothes and sighed some more. But he lifted one corner of the sheet and gave me an enormous wink.

Aunt Margaret can't resist a person in trouble. She can resist a parrot in trouble quite easily, but Harry Baggle was another matter. The next moment I heard her saying that, of course, she would look after the parrot personally.

"Only," she said with a frown, "how will I know *how* to look after him? I don't know anything about parrots."

"Well, he'll tell you, of course!" grinned the captain. "That *is* a weight off my mind. Would you like a choc?"

Later that afternoon, I went with Aunt Margaret to the Animal Rescue place. They seemed delighted to see us.

"Parrot Perkins? Such a character!" laughed the lady behind the desk, but it sounded a little false to me. I noticed that she backed towards the wall when one of the assistants brought in the parrot. I noticed a nasty look in his eye as well.

Aunt Margaret looked helplessly at the parrot. Just as the captain had promised, the parrot knew just what to do. He hopped on to Aunt Margaret's shoulder and stayed there, flexing his claws in a gentle but slightly menacing manner. I looked at him suspiciously. Now that I'd seen what a good actor the captain was, I was beginning to think that Parrot Perkins might be devious, too.

Back at her house, Aunt Margaret ran around putting old blankets over all the chair-backs. Parrot Perkins watched with something very close to a smile and examined his claws with care, holding up first one foot and then the other. Then he began to whistle.

The whistling gave Aunt Margaret an idea.

"Go and put the kettle on, darling, will you?" she said. "I'm parched, and I wouldn't mind a biscuit, too. It's ages since I had something to eat."

"*Something to eat!*" squawked the parrot, hopping about on a chair.

Aunt Margaret looked at him. Did he mean he was hungry, or was he just copying as he usually did?

"*Pleeeeease!*" said the parrot, which settled the matter.

It was rather fun sitting down to tea with Aunt Margaret and the parrot. Perkins turned out to like plain biscuits much better than the pink wafers that Aunt Margaret usually bought for me. When Aunt Margaret stretched out her hand for the last one, Parrot Perkins made his feelings known.

"*Tut, tut, tut!*" he said, and he sounded so much like Aunt Margaret that I laughed out loud. Even she hurriedly withdrew her hand from the plate and let the parrot lean down and peck up the last biscuit and some crumbs.

It was a few days later when I saw Aunt Margaret again. Usually, she was a plump, cheery-looking person. This was a completely new Aunt Margaret. She looked harassed. She looked worried. She even looked thinner. The expression on her face reminded me very much of the old lady who lost her favourite slippers.

"He's not a bad bird," she said, lowering her voice in case feathery ears were listening. "But he has such strong views about things. And it's no good me arguing or being firm. He simply won't listen. I feel as though he's taken over my life completely, from morning to night."

"*Night night!*" squawked the parrot and shut his eyes. To my astonishment, Aunt Margaret drew the curtains and switched off the lights, beckoning me to follow her into the kitchen.

"I have to do that," she explained. "When he wants to sleep, he wants to sleep, and he can't bear any noise or light. I haven't seen any of my favourite telly programmes all week. He likes to sleep in the living room, you see."

"But Cap'n Baggle used to take him up to bed with him, didn't he?" I asked, thinking it would be more convenient for Aunt Margaret's programmes.

She shuddered. "I did that the first night," she said, "and the comments he made about my nightclothes were hardly fit to hear. I hate to think what he'll tell the captain. It's a sorry thing when a woman can't feel at home in her own house. He interferes with everything I do. And do you know, he tore my favourite slippers to shreds, squawking *"Old, old, old!"* I tried to pull them away from him, but he was so determined. I mean, I *liked* those old slippers!"

I looked at Aunt Margaret. She looked at me. All of a sudden, a pink flush spread up from her neck to the roots of her hair.

"Oh!" she said. There was nothing else to say, really.

Aunt Margaret looked after Perkins Parrot for another six weeks, until Cap'n Baggle came out of hospital and settled back in his old home.

"You've obviously taken great care of him," said the captain, rubbing Perkins' beak. "I've never seen him looking better."

"Is there anything I can do to help you, Captain?" asked Aunt Margaret. "Of course, I won't interfere unless you ask me."

The captain looked up with a smile. "I've never seen you looking better either, Margaret," he said with a grin. "Why don't you wear turquoise more often? From what Perkins tells me…"

But Aunt Margaret was hurrying me out of the house.

"We mustn't linger," she said. "I'm sure the captain values his independence. What are you smiling at, child?"

The Ambitious Hippo

The River Mlabu is sluggish and a bit slimy. It's not the kind of place you would choose for a swim. In the mud at the bottom of the lazily swirling water, squiggly things squirm and wiggly things worm. Under the banks, beneath the drip, drip of the grey-green moss, crocodiles sleep until they ... *snap!* It is not, for humans, a healthy area to linger. But it was precisely here that Hepzibah Hippo chose to raise her family.

Hepzibah and her Homer had only one child. As a result, they doted on their daughter, whose name was Helen.

"Just look at those jaws," said the fond father. "She could sink a thousand ships any day."

"And her bottom is *huge*!" said her proud mother. A big bottom is a thing of beauty to a hippo, who, to be truthful, never ever have small bottoms.

Helen Hippo glowed beneath her parents' praise. Loved and cherished from the moment she was born, she was not lacking in confidence. Her parents were keen to encourage her to believe that anything was possible.

"Helen," they said, "when you grow up, you can be anything you want to be. All you have to do, darling, is believe in yourself and work hard. The sky's the limit. You are an amazing animal and a quite exceptional hippo. We feel sure that you will go far."

Helen Hippo was happy to hear all this. She believed every word of it. The only thing she had to do, she felt, was to work out what exactly she wanted to do. After that, actually doing it was a mere technicality.

For the first few years of her life, Helen was happy to wade and wallow. Things that squiggled and wiggled at the bottom of the river suffered badly under her fat little feet. Things that slept and snapped by the bank got tired of being bashed and barged when Helen heaved her great bulk out of the water every so often. Even the elephants that occasionally came to the river to drink steered clear of playful Helen. She once chomped into a dangling trunk, thinking it was a water snake, and elephants, as you know, have very long memories (especially when their trunks are a little short).

Helen, fortunately, was blissfully unaware that she was not the most popular animal in the area.

As Helen grew older (and heavier), she began to think it was time she had some ideas about what she would do with her life. Unfortunately, she was so very confident that these ideas were never in the least bit realistic.

Helen's first great passion was for dancing. She had seen graceful giraffes loping rhythmically over the plain. She had watched gazelles gambolling and prancing. Her mind was made up. She would be the greatest dancer in Africa— graceful, light-footed and untiring.

Three crushed frogs and a squashed warthog later, Helen was still convinced that her pirouettes were perfect and her leaps were legendary. To do her justice, she did practise at every opportunity. At first, her parents tried to encourage her.

"That was delightful, darling," they said, coughing as great clouds of dust were blown into their eyes by Helen's fiendish footwork. "It's wonderful to see so much ... *enthusiasm!*"

"Look!" cried Helen. "I can stand on tiptoes. Look! Oh ... oh ... oh ... I'm losing my balance ... *crash!*"

Helen's father was speechless. You would be speechless too if a large hippo landed on you.

"I'm going to try that again," said Helen, gamely lumbering to her feet and ignoring the pathetic wheezing and whimpering coming from her father.

After that, Hepzibah and Homer tended to keep clear when Helen was cavorting. They felt that they could see perfectly well from a distance.

To tell the truth, most of the local animals kept clear at such times. The snappy crocodiles swam out to the middle of the river, with only their eyes and noses showing above the murky water.

The warthogs hid behind bushes.

Even the elephants stood behind trees and tried to pretend they weren't there. It was hard to pretend with the earth shaking and the trees trembling from the force of Helen's hopping and skipping. Several wildebeest decided to set off early on their great trek northwards.

Helen might be crashing around the undergrowth to this day if she had not suddenly decided to take up medicine instead. It is hard to say where she got the idea from, but its results were even worse for the other animals.

Hippo feet are no more designed for delicate work with a syringe than they are for dancing. Helen was forced to use more vigorous methods to make her patients well again.

She chased an unfortunate flamingo around for several hours because she said he looked flushed. It took several more hours for her mother to persuade her that flamingos are naturally pink.

When Helen found a large snake groaning after a huge meal, she decided that there was only one way to deal with the enormous lump in his tummy. She jumped up and down on him. That snake has never been the same since.

When Homer Hippo found himself suffering from ingrowing toenails, he felt obliged to encourage his medical daughter by letting her nibble them away. Now, hippo teeth are designed for mighty munching and huge chomping. There is nothing careful or delicate about them. Poor Homer did not walk again for weeks. Helen bandaged his feet with the largest leaves she could find and was very disappointed when her father refused to undergo further treatment. Even fathers have their limits.

Setbacks like these—let's not even discuss the porcupine who lost his quills or the giraffe with a sore throat and the truly disastrous treatment they received from a hopeful hippo doctor—eventually persuaded Helen to think of another career. She decided to be a great writer.

Of course, hippos can't actually *write*, so what she really meant was that she would be a great storyteller, but she thought that *writer* sounded better. There is a great and noble tradition of story-telling among hippos. It was a career that her parents were, once again, very happy to encourage.

"This will be much more suitable," Hepzibah told her husband as he hobbled around on his healing toes. "I mean, how can she go wrong? Even if she is not the greatest storyteller in the world, she can't do anyone any physical *damage*."

Homer gave a hearty snort of relief. This was, indeed, much more suitable. Sadly, they were both wrong.

Now, you may feel that this story is lacking in pace and humour. You may not like the characters or the setting. You may have taken note of my name on the title page and made a firm and fervent decision never to read another book of mine as long as you live. But I can tell you (and I would have my hand on my heart if it wasn't tapping away at the computer keys) that this story is a heart-stopping helter-skelter of thrills and excitement compared with Helen's hippo tales. To say that her stories were boring hardly covers the stultifying sleepiness they caused.

A whole herd of gazelles drifted into a coma when Helen told her favourite story: *The Hippo and the Dung Heap.* Those that later woke up found that their numbers were much reduced. I'm afraid that several crafty lionesses had found that lurking on the edge of Helen's story circle was a much more efficient way of hunting than all the creeping and crouching and pouncing they usually did. Really, an unconscious gazelle is the lion equivalent of a fast-food outlet.

Before very long, several vultures joined Helen's sessions. She was impressed that she was drawing such a varied audience. The vultures, I'm afraid, grew so fat that they could hardly fly.

A few weeks later, after the most unfortunate disappearance of several more gazelles, wildebeest, flamingos and a baby elephant, a deputation from each group of animals (vegetarians only) arrived to speak to Hepzibah and Homer Hippo, who had not quite realized the full extent of the problem. (Well, they were asleep most of the time for obvious reasons, so they could hardly have been expected to notice.) They were surprised to see so many animals walking purposefully towards them.

"Mr. and Mrs. Hippo, this can't go on," said the largest elephant, who had been elected to speak. He was one of the few animals bigger and heavier than Homer and Hepzibah.

"This really is dreadful. We had no idea," cried the poor parents when the whole ghastly story was explained to them. "But how are we to persuade Helen to stop? She's ... er ... a strong-willed girl and very determined in all her many career choices."

"My friend the wildebeest here has a suggestion," boomed the elephant. "And I must say we all think it is a good one."

The wildebeest snickered with pride. "I knew your daughter would be reluctant to give up her storytelling," he said, "so I tried to think of a place where it wouldn't matter if listening animals went to sleep. It was very difficult, as some of us are in danger wherever we lay down our heads. But I suddenly had an inspiration. What about … the river?"

"The river?" For a moment, the hippo parents were puzzled. "But there's nothing in the river except squiggly things and wiggly things and crocodiles."

"Exactly," said the wildebeest. "Do we mind if anything happens to them?"

There was a short silence. Then…

"*Nah!*" chorused the elephant, the hippos, the flamingo, the gazelle and the warthog.

The next morning at breakfast, Homer played his part.

"How lucky all the animals are to be able to appreciate your talents, Helen," he said, "but sometimes I think it is a shame to entertain the privileged when there are so many creatures among us that need our help more urgently."

"Help?" Helen hadn't quite lost her doctor's zeal for helping people whether they wanted it or not.

"I'm thinking of the poor crocodiles," said Homer, shaking his head sadly.

Helen was surprised. "Poor" and "crocodiles" were not words that were usually heard together. In fact, she had never heard her father have a good word to say about crocodiles before. Although she had never paid much attention to those creatures herself, she had heard some very nasty stories from the other

animals (in the days when she let them get a word in edgeways). It had not occurred to her that crocodiles were in any way unfortunate.

"Just imagine," sighed Homer, wiping an imaginary tear from his eye, "what it must be like to be hated by everyone you meet. No wonder they lurk under the mossy bank. What else can they do, shunned by society and condemned to hide away from the world? If only some exceptional animal could bring a little life and colour into their drab existence. Sometimes I can't sleep at nights for thinking about it."

Helen, who had been woken by her father's vigorous snoring since she was a baby hippo, should have been suspicious at this point, but there is no one so single-minded as an artist who wants an audience.

"I can do it!" she cried. "I can bring joy to a dark world! I can bring light to a life without hope! I can bring happiness to a sad, gloomy existence!"

"Steady on!" said her father, without thinking. "I mean, please, please, dear daughter, don't overtax yourself. An artistic temperament like yours can be a delicate thing, my dear."

"There's no need to worry about me," said Helen cheerfully (and with accuracy). She took her artistic temperament off to the riverbank at once.

Well, the rest, as they say, is history. The poor crocodiles, at first deeply puzzled by a hippo who began droning on in the middle of the river, soon found themselves strangely fascinated. A little later, they all found themselves drowsy. Before long, each one of them was floating lazily, eyes shut, without a thought in the world of going ... *snap!*

With the crocodiles safely asleep, and Helen still droning interminably on, the other animals jumped in with a splash. They had a wonderful time, and the poor crocodiles slept through all of it. While deep on the bottom of the river, the wiggly things and the squiggly things didn't worm or squirm at all. They simply slept.

Lucy
Had a
Little Goat

Lucy lived on a farm. She liked all the animals but she knew that they had jobs to do. The cows gave milk early in the morning, long before Lucy was up, and in the afternoon. The hens laid eggs whenever they felt like it, but Lucy's mother collected them twice a day. The sheep had woolly coats that were sheared once a year. These animals didn't have individual names, and Lucy didn't think of them as pets.

Some other animals on the farm did have names. In the big barn, there lived three cats called Eeny, Meeny and Mo. Lucy's mother had told her that they were called that because she couldn't decide which to choose from the kittens of the last old cat and had ended up keeping all three of them. They ran about and caught all the mice they could, but they didn't come into the house.

Dad's dog Jip didn't come into the house, either, unless he wasn't well. He worked with Dad when he was looking after the sheep and was really clever at dealing with the silly sheep.

Lucy didn't think of the cats and the dog as pets either. They were just part of the busy life on the farm.

But when Lucy was old enough to go to school, she soon found that other children thought about their animals in a different way.

"I've got a hamster," said Tommy proudly. He sleeps a lot but at night he runs around and around on his little wheel. It's a bit squeaky. His name is Harry."

"Why do you have him?" asked Lucy. She had never heard of hamsters but she thought maybe they laid eggs or something. Although she couldn't really see the hens on the farm running around in a little wheel.

Tommy looked surprised. "He's a pet," he said. "I have him so that I can look after him and play with him."

Lucy understood about farming but she didn't really understand about pets.

"And then you eat him, I suppose," she said, matter of factly.

Tommy burst into tears and went to tell the teacher that Lucy was a horrible girl who wanted to eat his hamster. The teacher looked sharply at Lucy but said, "Oh no, Tommy, I'm sure that's not true. She knows that you love Harry. Have you asked her about her pets?"

Lucy frowned. "I help to take care of cows and sheep and hens," she said, "but I don't play with them and they don't have little wheels to run around."

That evening, the teacher had a word with Lucy's mother when she came to collect her. And when Lucy was tucked

up in bed much later, she read her a story about a little boy who had a pet rabbit. She explained to Lucy that children who didn't have animals around them all the time, as Lucy did, often liked to have an animal of their own at home.

"I wouldn't want a rabbit," said Lucy sleepily. "There are hundreds of them out in the field. And anyway, do they *like* being shut up like that?"

"Well, I don't know about that," said her mother. "I expect they like being looked after."

But Lucy was already asleep and dreaming of rabbits running around and around on little wheels.

Lucy didn't say much about it, but over the next few weeks she often thought about pets. She was still pretty puzzled about it. Another little boy at school had some fish in a tank. Lucy could see that it might be nice to stroke and feed a rabbit, who might wrinkle his nose in a cute way and look as if he was enjoying a lettuce leaf you had brought him. But what was the point of having fish? You couldn't stroke them. You couldn't tell if they were pleased to see you. Lucy shook her head. She couldn't understand it at all. She even wondered if perhaps they tasted good, but after the hamster incident she knew better than to ask.

Gradually, Lucy came to realize that almost *all* the children in the class had pets. One day in maths, the children had to cut out animals and put them on a chart to show which was the most popular pet. Most of Lucy's friends were cutting out cats and dogs and other small furry animals. Lucy decided against trying to cut out huge numbers of cows and sheep and hens. Anyway, she didn't think they counted. She cut out a picture of Jip instead and explained that he was her Dad's dog. That seemed to make everyone happy. Tommy, who hadn't spoken to her since the day they had discussed hamsters, sat next to her and helped her stick her picture on the chart.

That evening after supper, Lucy told her mother that she needed to have a pet.

"People like you better if you do," she explained.

"That's silly," said her mother, "but you can have a pet if you like. Only you will have to look after it all by yourself. We're too busy looking after the other animals to help. And remember, it's really important to look after animals properly. You know how Daddy feels about that."

"I will look after it," said Lucy. "Can we buy one this weekend?"

"Not this weekend, darling," said her mother. "We're going to the County Show, remember? Next weekend we will think about it."

But Lucy simply couldn't get pets off her mind, and perhaps that is why although three members of the family went to the County Show, four members came back. The newcomer was a goat!

"Are you sure, sweetheart?" Lucy's dad had asked. "This little chap is very young, but goats get big. You won't be able to bring him in the house."

"I know. That's okay," said Lucy. "I just think he has a little tiny bit of all the animals I like best in him. He's black and white like the cows. His face is a little bit like a sheep's. And he's got bright little eyes like the hens."

So that was that.

"And I'm going to call him Gordon," said Lucy. She couldn't understand why her mother and father burst out laughing, even when they said they knew someone called Gordon themselves.

"Anyone would be glad to share a name with my Gordon," she said.

Over the next few weeks, Lucy's dad suggested several new names for her Gordon, and not all of them were polite.

"Guzzler, would be a better name," he said. "Or Greedyguts. Or Gulper. Or Gorger. Or, wait a minute, what about Gobbler?"

"It's natural for a young goat to be hungry," said Lucy. "Gordon is growing."

Gordon certainly was growing. But he was also a guzzler, a gorger, a gulper, a gobbler and a greedyguts. He ate anything he could reach, from Lucy's mother's old gardening gloves, left on the fence, to half of one of her father's boots, left outside to dry. As for the flowers and shrubs that struggled to grow around the farmhouse, their struggle was over. Gordon ate them, and that was that.

When Gordon attacked the laundry, flapping in the breeze one sunny morning, Lucy's mother put her foot down.

"That goat has to be kept further away from the house," she said. "We will tether him in the orchard. You can move him each day so that he always has fresh new grass to munch. He will be happy and our underwear will be safe."

Gordon was certainly very happy in the orchard. The grass was delicious there. But Gordon soon found other ways of getting food. He realized that if he butted the trees hard with his head (and his head was extremely hard), little green apples and plums and pears would tumble down. Gordon didn't mind that they were green, but as time passed and the fruit began to ripen, he enjoyed it even more. And it seemed to fall off much more easily, too.

One summer evening, Lucy's parents wandered out into the orchard to see how their crop was doing. Lucy went along too, to find out how Gordon was doing. The farmer and his wife searched high and low, but all they found were two very shrivelled apples that refused to fall from their branch, a rotten plum and three pears right at the top of their tree. It was all too clear who the culprit was. Gordon wasn't very good at his "Who? Me?" act.

"Well, it's too late now," said the farmer. "But we'll have to find a new home for him next year."

He meant that they must find another place for Gordon to be tethered, but Lucy, waiting discreetly behind a tree in case there was any shouting, heard this with horror. She thought her father meant Gordon must leave the farm. Right there and then she decided to hide him.

It's not easy to hide a goat. It's even more difficult to hide a hungry goat. That evening, when both her parents were inside the house, Lucy tried putting Gordon in the old stable. But next morning, when she crept out before breakfast to take him some cornflakes, she found that he had chewed through the rotting wood of the old door and was back in the flowerbeds doing his worst. Lucy hurriedly pulled him away and shut him in the big barn instead. It was a huge mistake. Let loose with dozens of sacks of grain, Gordon had a wonderful time.

By the end of the day, when a large chunk of a haystack, a bag of beans, some chickenfeed and a bucket of whitewash had all been consumed by Gordon in various hiding places, Lucy was convinced that there was nowhere on the farm to hide him safely. Perhaps that is why she had the outrageous idea of taking him to school.

School was not very far away, and Lucy was allowed to walk there by herself as she could go all the way along paths beside the fields of her own farm. The next morning, she set off earlier than usual, telling her mother that there was a special visitor at school that day.

"I know," said her mother rather unexpectedly. "I hope you like him. Have a good day!"

Lucy knew that she would never be able to smuggle Gordon unseen into school, but she hoped that she could pretend that she had brought him along to show her friends. Then maybe her teacher would let her leave him on the playing field until it was time to go home.

But things did not go according to plan. Because she had set off much earlier than usual, there was no one about when she came into the playground. The school caretaker had already opened the school and was busy doing something in his shed at the back, but there were no children in sight. Lucy was trying to decide what to do, when the heavens opened and it began to rain heavily. Without thinking, she pulled open the door and pushed Gordon inside. Lucy had never been in the school when it was empty before. With Gordon by her side, she wandered down the long corridors and peeped into classrooms she didn't usually see. But all the while, in the back of her mind, she was wondering what to do about Gordon. He looked horribly conspicuous.

Suddenly, coming around the next corner, Lucy heard footsteps. Someone was here already, and from the heavy tread of the feet, it must be one of the teachers. Lucy panicked. She opened the nearest door and pushed Gordon inside, then strolled down the corridor trying to look as innocent as possible.

"Hello, Lucy, you're early today," said her teacher.

That morning, Lucy could hardly concentrate at all. She wondered what Gordon was doing. She wondered if he was safe. She had pushed him into one of the storerooms on the other side of the corridor, but it wasn't until morning break that several horrible thoughts struck her all at once. What, she wondered, if the storeroom didn't have a window? What if

it didn't have enough air? What if Gordon was suffocating?

Lucy knew that she had been very silly. She was almost in tears as she rushed up to her teacher and explained that her Gordon must be rescued at once.

It took ages for the teacher to start to understand what Lucy was saying.

"A goat?" he asked. "In a cupboard? Are you sure, Lucy?"

"Yes, yes!" It was clear from Lucy's distraught face that something was badly wrong. The teacher took hold of the little girl's hand and said gently, "Why don't you show me?"

Out in the corridor, Lucy stood with her teacher in front of the cupboard door. There was no sound from inside. Lucy hardly dared open the door. The teacher stretched out his hand and turned the knob.

There *was* a window inside! There was a goat, too, peacefully asleep on the floor. And there was the most dreadful mess you have ever seen. Half-eaten books were heaped all over the floor. There didn't seem to be one without nibbled pages or a huge chunk bitten out of the cover.

"Oh no!" wailed Lucy. "Oh Gordon, what have you done?"

"Did I hear my name?" asked an amused voice behind her.

Lucy and the teacher turned. The scene in the cupboard was horrifying, but this was worse. Standing there with expressions of astonishment were the headmaster and a strange man—a Very Important Visitor who was being shown around the school.

"Mr. Miles," said the headmaster, "I can assure you that this sort of thing has *never* happened before. I know that you would not want to make the generous donation you are suggesting if you thought that we allowed *this* sort of thing. I promise you…"

But the man was bending down and smiling broadly.

"I think you must be Lucy," he said. "And I'm very much afraid this must be my namesake, Gordon. Your parents told me that you had chosen an excellent name for your goat!"

"Well, shall we…?" The headmaster was still trying to smooth over the situation.

But Gordon Miles was laughing as Gordon the goat, hearing the noise, woke up and at once started chewing a copy of *Transport Through the Ages*. It didn't, however, seem to appeal to him very much, for he dropped it at once and began on *Five Hundred Famous Physicians*.

"These books appear to appeal to goats as much as to children," said the Very Important Visitor. "I think I'll have to increase my donation to cover what Gordon here has saved you the trouble of throwing away. Now, Lucy, why don't I help you take him home?"

The Perfect Polar Bear

If you ask anyone what colour a polar bear is, he or she will reply without the slightest hesitation.

"Is this some kind of trick? They're white, of course!"

Everyone knows that snow is white, and that the fur of polar bears helps to camouflage them in the snowy wastes of the Arctic Circle. So polar bears must be white. Right?

Wrong! If you have ever seen a polar bear, you will know that it wouldn't win any washing-powder whiteness prizes. Its fur is a kind of dirty, creamy, yellowy colour. Those pristine white fluffy bears you can buy for babies are way off the mark. Polar bears are shaggy and grubby, and no kind of advertisement for the purity of the icy world of the North Pole.

If you think about it, it stands to reason. How do polar bears keep clean in the Arctic? Do they jump under a hot shower when their fur gets grubby? Do they toddle down to the Polar Bear Beauty Parlour when they want to go just a little bit blonder? No, of course not. The only place they have for a good wash is the Atlantic Ocean. It's not a brilliant turquoise like the Caribbean. It's not a shimmering blue like the Mediterranean.

It's grey. And not a very clean-looking grey at that.

You can't really blame the sea, either. How can a piece of water that's packed with fish, and seals, and the oily hulls of fishing boats possibly keep clean? I don't like to mention it, but every one of those swimmers and floaters is using the sea for *all* its biological functions. Know what I mean? Let's not talk any more about it. It will put you off your fishfingers.

So, as I say, it's no one's fault, really, that polar bears are not white. You can't blame those bears at all. I'm sure they do their best to keep clean in very difficult conditions. And, come to think of it, you don't often hear of Arctic explorers taking baths either, do you? In fact, the North

Pole is a good deal
smellier and dirtier
than you might
think.

Polar bears,
I'm happy to say,
are unaware of any
lack of personal
hygiene among their friends and relations.
And you can be sure that none of the
smaller animals is going to say a word.
They all live in fear of polar bears, who are
bigger, stronger, faster and fiercer than
anyone else on the ice. The only living
creatures that polar bears have to worry
about are humans, and most of them
would rather sit at home in warm sitting
rooms, watching polar bears on television,
than venture into the freezing wastes of
Greenland and all points north. Which is
just as well for the polar bears.

This story concerns a polar bear family with a difference. Pellida and Paolo Polar Bear got together one long dark winter and found that they had a lot in common—ice, fur, black noses, and a love of fresh cod (uncooked and preferably in large quantities). With so many shared interests, it wasn't surprising that they soon decided to make things permanent. Not long after that, they decided to start a family of their own.

Pellida dug herself a beautiful ice-cave and settled down to await the arrival of her cubs. Paolo was most attentive, bringing little treats of fish-heads and seal-livers whenever she was peckish. It doesn't sound attractive to us, but these are the red roses and champagne of the polar bear world. Pellida looked smug and Paolo was proud and happy.

He was even prouder and happier the day that Pellida produced two fine cubs. The pleased parents decided to call the little girl Pearl and the boy Pedro. They were very cute, fluffy, cuddly cubs, soon surrounded by adoring aunts and uncles with lots of useless advice on the raising of fine, upstanding bears.

Later, much later, Pellida and Paolo wondered if they had made a mistake in naming their daughter Pearl. After all, a pearl is a lustrous, white, gleaming jewel. A polar bear, an ordinary polar bear, is a shaggy, hairy, creamy, yellowish animal.

But they were not to know what was going to happen.

Polar bear cubs are, of course, not as shaggy, hairy, creamy or yellowish as their parents. Their fur is fluffy and clean. You still couldn't really say it is white, not in the way that white bathtubs and white toothpastes are white, but they are a lot whiter than their parents. Pearl was still very, very young when she realized this, and she felt pretty pleased to be so clean and pretty compared with her mother.

At this stage, the cubs were still in their ice-cave. The cave, after being lived in for several months and suffering as the scene of several fish-head suppers, was not very gleaming and pristine either. That is why, the first time that Pearl found out what whiteness really is like was the first time her mother led her out of the cave into the fresh, sparkling snow and ice outside. Pearl simply couldn't believe it.

"Mummy, Mummy, help!" she cried, as her brother ran off to play in the snow. "I'm all dirty, look!"

Pellida looked, but all she could see was a perfectly normal polar bear cub standing in some perfectly normal snow.

"No, you're not," she said. "You look fine. What's the matter?"

But Pearl was genuinely distressed. "Look!" she cried again. And she showed Pellida her little fluffy paw against the whiteness of the snow. Certainly, the cold stuff was a lot whiter than Pearl's little paw, but Pellida still couldn't see what the problem was. It took a long time for Pearl, who hadn't been taught how to talk about colours in the cave, to explain what she was worried about.

Pellida looked perplexed. She really couldn't see what all the fuss was about, but if the little one really felt she wasn't clean, then a dip in the ocean was the answer to all her problems.

"Come along," said Pellida. "You'll soon be clean. It's time you both learnt to swim, anyway." And she led the way to the edge of the ice, where the waters of the Atlantic Ocean slapped and slopped against the towering sides of icebergs.

"You'll both be excellent swimmers," said Pellida. "All you have to do is jump in. Look, I'll show you!"

With an almighty splash, Pellida plopped into the water. There was plenty of time, she thought, to show her cubs the finer points of diving.

Pedro hesitated for a moment. Then he ran towards the edge on his little furry feet. Just before he got there, he changed his mind and slammed on the brakes, but it was too late. His four paws settled into a skid and shot him inexorably towards the water. His splash was much smaller than his mother's, but the result was the same. In another moment he was bobbing around happily in the water and waving to his sister.

"Come on in, Pearl!" he called. "It's lovely! And it's not cold at all!"

Pearl stood aghast on the ice.

"You must be joking!" she shuddered. "I'm not coming into that filthy water. It's even greyer and dingier than I am! There's no way I'm ever going in."

Pellida frowned. A polar bear who can't swim is a polar bear who can't eat. You can wait for a long time for a seal to be silly enough to haul itself up on the ice and sit there looking like dinner.

Paolo had been watching from the shore and saw Pellida's distress.

"Don't worry," he said. "She'll get used to it. I'll take her for a brisk roll in the snow instead. You have a long swim with Pedro. And if you happen to come across some fat cod while you're there…"

Pearl was happy to roll in the snow, but after that all she wanted to do was to sit down and lick her claws clean. In the end, Paolo made sure she was in a safe place and went off to check on the cod-catching situation.

The polar bear parents were hopeful that Pearl's problem with the ocean would pass, but it didn't. In time, Pedro became a very fine cod-catcher. He could dive, swim and glide underwater with grace and speed. He tried hard to persuade his sister that it was fun.

"On land," he said, "we're sort of big and lumbering. But underwater, we're as speedy as fish. You'd really like it."

Pearl shook her head. "You speak for yourself," she said. "*I* don't lumber on land. And I have *never* wanted to be at all like a fish. They're smelly!"

Pearl's view of the ocean didn't change—until the day that she and her mother frightened away a fisherman sitting patiently beside a hole in the ice. Pearl peered down into the hole and was just about to turn away in disgust at the sight of a pool full of grey water when ... she noticed that it was full of her! Unlike the restless water on the coast, the water in the hole was almost still, and Pearl could see a beautiful reflection of herself peering back at her. She thought she looked pretty good. No matter what her mother said, Pearl refused to move on. She stared in fascination at her reflection, turning her face in a vain attempt to see what the back of her head looked like. She was terribly disappointed when, a few hours later, the hole iced over.

It wasn't long before Pearl's attitude caused serious problems in the polar bear family. It wasn't that she was lazy. She was quite happy to help dig ice-caves, as long as the ice wasn't so hard it scratched her claws. But Pearl simply refused to go fishing. At first, Pedro was proud to bring the fish he had caught to his sister. She had just as big an appetite as he had. But after a while he began to feel that it was unfair.

"She doesn't catch them. Why should she eat them?" he asked his father.

Paolo wrinkled his nose. "You have a point, my son," he said, "but what's the alternative? We can't let your sister starve."

"Why not?" asked Pedro coldly. "Anyway, I don't think she would. I think she'd start swimming straight away once she got hungry."

Paolo talked the matter over with Pellida that evening.

"He could be right," he said. "We could give it a try."

Pellida was reluctant to see her daughter suffer, but she agreed. Looking to the future, she was afraid that a polar bear who couldn't fish would never find a husband and raise a family of her own.

The next morning, Pellida explained to Pearl that she would have to do her own fishing from now on.

Pearl simply didn't understand. "But I can't," she said.

"Then you will have to go hungry," replied Pellida, hardening her heart.

After that, Paolo, Pellida and Pedro ate their meals in the water.

Pearl watched from the ice for a while. Her tummy began to rumble. She peered down into the grey water. Could she? No! Would she? No! She turned on her heel and walked away across the ice and snow with as much dignity as she could muster. She already felt a little faint from lack of fish but she had had an idea.

Over the next few days, Pellida kept a close eye on her daughter whenever she was herself out of the water. A polar bear can only last so long without food. But Pearl showed no signs of flagging. He coat was as thick and her eyes were as bright as ever. In fact, if anything, Pearl was looking a little happier than usual. It was strange.

Days passed. Weeks passed. Pearl went from strength to strength. She was growing up now, and some of the young male bears were beginning to follow her around with silly smiles on their faces.

"I believe I've solved the mystery," Pellida told Paolo. "That young minx is probably getting her admirers to fish for her. No wonder she isn't getting thinner."

But Paolo shook his head. "Male bears are taught from an early age," he said, "that the first thing you should look for in a wife is good fishing skills. I've had words with Pedro about it myself. A black nose and shining eyes are no use at all if a lady bear can't fish. Take it from me, those bears are not fishing for Pearl. I've had a horrible thought, though. What if she is *stealing* fish from other bears?"

Pellida was horrified. She didn't want to think that her daughter was a thief. Two minutes' thought made her feel a little calmer.

"That's silly," she said. "Where would she be stealing fish *from*? All the other polar bears are like us. They eat their fish fresh, as soon as they have caught them. They don't leave them lying about for another bear to steal. No, there is only one explanation. She must just be too proud to let us know that we were right. She has to be waiting until we are

asleep and then slipping into the water by herself and doing her own fishing then."

"Well, there's only one way to find out," said Paolo. "We'll have to watch her and see what she does."

Polar bears are not really built for undercover surveillance. Paolo's attempts to pretend to be an iceberg when watching his daughter were pretty pathetic. But there really isn't anything else you can pretend to be in the Arctic. Paolo's seal-impressions were impossibly bad.

Paolo's ability to stay awake was impossibly bad, too. After three nights when he had to confess to Pellida that he had failed to watch his daughter for more than an hour or two, Pellida decided to join him. Frankly, two large polar bears pretending to be icebergs are no more convincing than one, but at least Pellida was able to nudge Paolo each time he started to snore.

The anxious parents waited for what seemed like hours. Pearl simply did what all self-respecting polar bears were doing at that time. She slept. Paolo slept too, in between nudges. Pellida got fed up.

"I'm hungry!" she hissed to Paolo. "Let's go and get some breakfast!"

"Good idea!" whispered Paolo with relief. "I couldn't sit here a moment longer. I don't know how those icebergs stand it."

For a polar bear capable of making such a very silly remark, Paolo's next thought was remarkably sensible.

"Me meen mimiots!" he shouted, bobbing to the surface with a fish in his mouth. When he had swallowed the fish, he made more sense.

"We've been idiots! This is when she does her fishing—while we are! She must just do it somewhere else. If we creep back on to the ice, we'll catch her coming back and get an idea of the general direction," he said.

Back on shore, Pellida and Paolo trotted to the top of an ice hill to look around. When they spotted Pearl, they could hardly believe their eyes. She *was* fishing, but she wasn't getting her fur wet. She was using the line left behind by the fleeing angler to fish through a hole in the ice—and admire her own reflection at the same time. She was oblivious to the young male bears who sat admiringly at a respectful distance.

Pellida and Paolo sighed.

"Who says beauty and brains don't go together?" asked Pellida.

"That's my girl," grinned Paolo.